Amy HODGEPODGE
ALL MIXED UP!

BY KIM WAYANS & KEVIN KNOTTS
ILLUSTRATED BY SOO JEONG

SCHOLASTIC INC.
New York Toronto London Auckland Sydney
Mexico City New Delhi Hong Kong Buenos Aires

For Elvira, Howell, Billie, and Ivan.
And for Sylvia—the best teacher ever.

ISBN-13: 978-0-545-10904-8
ISBN-10: 0-545-10904-3

12 11 10 9 8 7 6 5 4 3 2 1   8 9 10 11 12 13/0

Printed in the U.S.A.   40

First Scholastic printing, September 2008

Chapter 1

"Amy," Mom called from downstairs. "Hurry up. You're going to be late for school."

I loved hearing that word—*school*. No, I'm not weird or anything. It's just that I've never been to school before. Not a real one, anyway. My mom, grandma, and grandpa have homeschooled me since I was really little. And boy, was I excited to start fourth grade in an actual school. (Okay, and a bit nervous, too.)

Dad always says there's a first time for everything. I guess he's right. He says sometimes you have to take a chance and do something you've never done before. You can't be afraid to change.

And that's just what my family had done. Made a change. A big one! We moved all the way across the country, from the tiny little town where I was born to our new house in Maple Heights, a neighborhood in Dyver City. We moved because Dad got a job at the brand-new Children's Hospital downtown. He's a pediatrician. A really good one, if you ask me.

"Amy!"

"I'm coming!" I yelled as I put away the scrapbook page that I was working on. Scrapbooking was one of my favorite hobbies. It all started when my grandmother gave me some beautiful handmade paper. Ever since then, I've kept a scrapbook filled with photos, letters, and all sort of keepsakes that remind me of happy memories. My scrapbook already had a picture of my new school. I couldn't wait to fill up the rest of the pages with new memories of all the friends I would make and fun I would have at school.

I took one last look at myself in my full-length mirror. I had tried on five other outfits that morning, but I decided to wear my favorite dress. It was the pretty one Mom and Dad had bought for me on our family vacation to Hawaii. The dress has lots of beautiful colors and a big pink flower that snaps onto the shoulder.

My Family

Obaasan
(Grandma)

Harabujy
(Grandpa)

Me!

Giggles

Mom

Dad

My new school!
(Emerson Charter School)

I ♥
Giggles

As soon as I put it on I was sure every kid in the school would love my dress, especially when they found out where I'd gotten it. I'd be a big hit!

By the time I got downstairs, Mom, Dad, and my grandparents were already eating breakfast. My grandparents weren't just visiting. They lived with us all the time.

"Well, don't you look beautiful today?" Dad said with a smile.

"Are you *sure* you want to wear that dress, Amy?" Mom asked.

For some reason, she wasn't smiling. It had taken me a long time to convince my parents that I should stop being homeschooled. Had she changed her mind? Or maybe she really just didn't like my dress.

"It's my favorite dress!" I said.

"Okay," Mom said with a sigh. "Come and have some breakfast. You have to be at the bus stop in twenty minutes."

I sat down next to my grandmother. But before I could reach for my cereal, she put her hand over mine and said, "Little Mitsukai, I'm going to miss you all day."

My grandmother was born in Japan and she always called me Little Mitsukai. Little Angel.

My grandfather didn't speak Japanese. He was from Korea. And he didn't have a nickname for me at all. He always said there was no need for nicknames when I had a perfectly nice name already.

Dad's parents are like that, too. Different. His mother is black and his father is white. Sometimes when we're all together—my parents, grandparents, aunts, uncles, and cousins—I wonder if people will even know we are a family since we all look so different from one another.

"I'll be back at three, Obaasan," I said to my grandmother. "And we can go for our daily walk then, okay?"

She nodded and poured a little more tea for herself and my grandfather even though his teacup was still half full. They both loved tea. *A lot.*

"So, are you sure you want to go to school?" Dad asked. There was a little worry-wrinkle in his forehead.

"I'm sure," I answered. But there were lots of butterflies in my stomach. I just didn't want anyone to know about them.

Hearing this, Mom sighed again. Sometimes it felt like nobody in my family wanted me to go to a regular school. They wanted me to stay home and learn from them because they still had a lot they wanted to teach me.

But I wanted to change. I was tired of spending every day at home with Mom, my grandparents, and my dog, Giggles. I wanted real, non-dog friends. I wanted to sit with my friends at lunch and share jokes, play tag, and jump rope with them at recess. I wanted to get invited to birthday parties and sleepovers on the weekends.

Sometimes I thought my parents would never understand that.

After breakfast, I spent a few minutes in the

yard playing with Giggles. He has honey-brown fur and lopsided ears.

But that's not why I love him so much. I love him because he's friendly and huggable. The perfect dog, really. That's why I felt so guilty for leaving him. He would probably miss me the whole time I was at school. And I knew I would miss him, too.

Finally it was time to leave and Dad came outside. "I'll take you to the bus stop and then go straight to work once you get on the bus," he said.

"Okay, Dad. But you can just drop me off. You don't have to wait around for the bus to come," I told him.

"Don't be silly," Dad said. "I wouldn't miss seeing you step onto the school bus for the first time."

I pet Giggles one last time. He jumped into my arms and licked my face.

"Phew, Giggles," I said. "Your breath stinks. You need to lay off the liver biscuits."

Then I led him back into the house. I couldn't help feeling a little worried. I didn't want to be the only one waiting at the bus stop with my father. How embarrassing would that be?

Chapter 2

I was embarrassed, all right.

As soon as Dad's car pulled up to the corner of Eighteenth Street and Walnut Avenue, I saw a group of kids standing at the bus stop. And there wasn't one parent in sight.

"Are you ready?" Dad asked me, turning off the car engine.

I nodded slowly.

I got out of the car and smoothed down my dress. The kids at the bus stop all looked like they were having a good time. One girl was wearing a T-shirt that said "I Rode the Monster Loop Roller Coaster" and talking to a friend. A few other girls were singing and clapping their hands together. I wished I knew how to play hand-clapping games like that. It looked like a lot of fun.

❀ 11 ❀

I also wished that I knew at least one other kid at the bus stop. It was hard enough to go to school for the first time, but it was even harder because I was starting in the middle of the year. Everyone else already had a few months to get to know one another and make friends.

"I sure hope this bus comes soon," Dad said

loudly. "I need to get to the hospital on time."

All the kids at the bus stop turned and stared at us. I could feel my face getting hot. "It's okay if you leave, Dad," I whispered. "I'll see you later."

But even as I said it, a little part of me wanted him to stay. Just this once. I didn't want to stand there by myself with all those kids who already knew one another.

After what seemed like an hour, the bus finally came. I ran up the steps before Dad could kiss me good-bye. I felt a little bad about that, but I didn't want to be even more embarrassed. The kids were already staring at me enough.

I walked down the bus aisle, hoping to find an empty seat. The only one left was all the way in the back, next to a large boy with a crew cut.

As soon as I sat down, the boy turned to me and said, "I never saw you on this bus before. Are you new?"

"Yeah," I said. Then I worked up the courage to introduce myself. "I'm Amy Hodges. What's your name?"

He didn't answer me. He just smiled slyly and said, "I *knew* you were new."

That didn't go so well, I thought. But at least I had actually talked to somebody. That was a big improvement over what had happened at the bus stop.

After we had gone a few blocks, the boy opened his notebook and started writing something. I couldn't see what he was doing because he covered the page with his hand. Since he didn't seem like he wanted to talk, I looked around at all the other kids that were talking and laughing with one another.

I wished that I had something to do since no one seemed interested in talking to me.

So I opened up my notebook and looked at an article from *The Dyver City Times* that I had pasted inside. It was about my new school, Emerson Charter School. Every time I read the article I got more excited. Emerson was different than other schools. Sure, you learned stuff like reading and math, but you also had cool classes like music, dance, and drama, and—

Ooof! Suddenly, I felt a hard slap on my back.

"Ow!" I cried.

"Sorry," the boy next to me said, but he had a smile on his face. "I just wanted to pat you on the back and welcome you to Emerson Charter School, that's all."

"Um, thanks," I mumbled. My back was still tingling with pain.

I didn't think he meant to hurt me. He was probably trying to be nice. Maybe he just didn't know his own strength.

Chapter 3

When the bus stopped in front of the school, all the kids jumped up out of their seats. I didn't want to rush, so I waited until everyone was off before I got up.

"Are you Amy Hodges?" a girl asked me as soon as I stepped off the bus.

"Yes," I said, nervously. How did she know who I was?

"I'm Liza Toddley," she said, peering at me through her thick glasses. "We're in the same class, and our teacher made, um, I mean, *asked* me to show you around the school and make sure you get to the right classroom."

I smiled. The day was starting to get better!

"That's an *interesting* dress you're wearing,"

Liza said, playing with her ponytail. Well, it wasn't exactly a ponytail. She had a bunch of tiny braids gathered together tightly in a hair tie on the top of her head. It looked like it hurt. I bet she was going to have a terrible headache by the end of the day.

"Thanks," I said. "I got it in Hawaii."

Liza led me up the front steps and into the school building. She was tall and had very long legs, which meant that she walked pretty fast. I had to practically run to keep up with her.

As we walked through the halls it felt like everyone's eyes were on me. I thought I had even heard somebody laughing.

"Here is the library," Liza said. "Our class comes here twice a week to work on our reports. I always sit with my friend Jennifer, but I'm sure *someone* will sit with you."

"Uh-oh," Liza whispered. "Here comes trouble." She pointed toward the boy who I sat next to on the bus.

"Him?" I whispered back. "He was sort of nice to me on the bus."

"Rory isn't nice to anybody," Liza said.

"Hey, girls," Rory said with a weird grin on

his face. As he walked passed us, I heard him snicker and say, "Good. It's still there."

What was he talking about? *What* was still there?

"Forget about him," Liza said, waving her hand in the air. Then she continued her tour. "This is the gym. And across the hall is the cafeteria. I would eat with you, but I always have lunch with Jennifer."

Who was this Jennifer, anyway? But before I got the chance to ask her, she reached out and grabbed a doorknob. "And this is our classroom. You're lucky. We have the best teacher in the whole school, Mrs. Clark."

When I stepped inside I saw Mrs. Clark standing in front of the room writing on the blackboard. I couldn't see her face, but the first thing I noticed was her hair. It was brown with silver streaks, and it reached all the way down her back. Not only was her hair long, but so was her cool skirt. It almost touched the floor.

There were a lot of kids in the classroom,

too. I recognized some of them from the bus. Most of the kids in the class were talking to one another. Some were in the back of the room feeding the fish or cleaning the hamster cage. The whole room was practically buzzing—just what I'd been looking forward to.

"Let me show you where your desk is," Liza said. I walked with her down the aisle nearest the windows. "This is your desk," Liza told me. "You're right behind me."

I smiled and took a seat at my desk. As I got settled, I noticed Liza leaning over to talk to a blond girl in the next row. "Hey, Jennifer," she whispered a little too loudly. "Check out the dress the new girl is wearing. Isn't it horrible?"

"*Worse* than horrible," Jennifer replied. "And that big flower on her shoulder is so ugly!"

Then they both laughed. They didn't even try to hide it!

I was shocked. I could feel my eyes filling up with hot tears. Why were they being so mean? What had I ever done to them?

I reached over and grabbed the flower on my shoulder and pulled on it hard. I thought I would hear it unsnap, but instead I heard a loud *RIP*. The flower was in my hand, and my beautiful dress was ruined. And now there wasn't any way to hide the big, giant hole.

When Mrs. Clark finished writing on the board, she knelt beside my desk. "Amy, welcome to my fourth-grade class. I'm Mrs. Clark." She had a nice smile on her face and that helped me feel a lot more comfortable.

"Hi," I said, blinking back my tears. Then I put on a big, fake smile. I didn't want my teacher to think I was a baby on my first day of school.

Mrs. Clark stood up and then walked to the front of the room.

"Class, as I'm sure you have all noticed, we have a new student. Amy, please come to the front of the room and tell everyone a little about you," said Mrs. Clark.

Me? In front of the classroom? And now

wearing a ripped-up dress? I was starting to panic.

"Amy?" Mrs. Clark said again, motioning for me to get up.

As I walked to the front of the room, my face felt hot and my heart was beating at triple speed.

Then I heard some of the kids giggling. Everybody had probably noticed that my dress was ripped. Could things get any worse?

When I got to the front of the room, Mrs. Clark stood beside me and said, "Go ahead, Amy."

"Um," I started, shifting from one foot to the other. All I wanted to do was run away. Run right out of the classroom, out of the school, and just keep running until I got back home again.

It took me a few seconds to start talking. In a very low voice I said, "I'm new in town." My head felt like it was a big balloon filled with helium. "I was homeschooled my whole

life. Until now. And, uh, I have a dog named Giggles." I stopped. I was way too nervous to think of anything else to say.

"Well, thank you, Amy," Mrs. Clark said, smiling. "And welcome to Emerson."

"Thank you," I said and started to walk back to my seat.

But before I could move, Mrs. Clark put her hand on my shoulder. "What is this?" she asked, pulling off a large piece of paper that had been stuck to my back with tape.

"*Stupid new girl*," she read then looked up at the class. She looked really angry. "Who put this on Amy's back? I want an answer right now."

All of the kids looked around at one another, but nobody answered Mrs. Clark. They didn't have to. I knew exactly who had put that sign on my back. Rory. He must have done it when he slapped me on the bus. And that was why he had laughed when he saw me in the hallway and said something about "it" still being there.

What I didn't understand was why he had done it. He had only just met me. Why would he make fun of me? And how could I have been so stupid to think he was being nice?

From now on I had to watch out for people like Rory. And Liza and Jennifer. If this was what school was all about, I was ready to go back to being homeschooled. At least everybody liked me at home.

Chapter 4

   The next few hours went by in a blur. After Mrs. Clark took attendance, we got right down to work. First we had reading, then history.

   Even though I was interested in what Mrs. Clark was saying, I just couldn't sit still. I just wasn't used to sitting at a desk all day. I felt like I had ants in my pants! When I was homeschooled, my grandmother and I went on daily walks and discussed current events. My grandfather and I would study history together. We would go to the library and check out books and documentaries and sometimes go to museums. And before we moved to Maple Heights, Mom and I belonged to a mother-daughter book club. That was a lot of fun, too.

As I sat at my desk, I wiggled my left foot, then my right. I stretched my neck and shook my hands.

"Hey, could you please stop moving around?" the kid sitting behind me whispered.

For the rest of the lesson I sat perfectly still. I barely even breathed!

Finally, it was time to go to music class. All the kids lined up by the front door. I stood up a little too late and got stuck standing right behind Liza and Jennifer. *Great*, I thought as Liza and Jennifer looked at me and giggled. *Aren't there any nice kids in the class?*

Mrs. Clark walked with us down the hall to a large room that was decorated with cutouts of musical notes and posters of famous composers. There was a piano in front of the room and lots of other instruments in cases everywhere.

It was so cool! I wanted to look at everything in the room and try all of the instruments at once. But before I could do anything, another group of kids came into the room. Their teacher was a lot older than Mrs. Clark. She wore dark red lipstick and her hair was pulled into a tight bun.

"Hurry up, hurry up," she said to her class in a thick accent. "Take your places." She sounded like a neighbor I used to have who was from Russia.

Mrs. Clark said hello to the other teacher— her name was Mrs. Musgrove.

After both teachers left, all the kids gathered around the piano. Everyone seemed to know exactly what to do, except me. I was so confused that I couldn't even find a good place to stand.

"Good morning, everyone," the music teacher said. He was tall and thin and had long, stringy hair.

"Good morning, Mr. Ship," everyone said together.

Mr. Ship took a seat at the piano and started playing. "Let's begin by working on 'Feeling Free,' the song we started learning last week," he said as his fingers ran up and down the black-and-white keys.

While the class practiced the song, I tried to learn the words and melody. By the third time they sang the song, I was able to join in. I started singing quietly at first, but before I knew it I was singing louder and louder. I closed my eyes and let my whole body feel the words and music. "If I could," I sang. "I would be free . . ."

I kept singing until it felt like I was the only one in the room. ". . . like a bird in the—" I was concentrating so hard that I could only hear my own voice.

And there was a good reason for that—I was the only one singing!

I opened my eyes quickly. Not only had everyone else stopped singing, but they were all staring right at me. And most of them were smiling. Were they all laughing at me?

I was so embarrassed that my cheeks must have been bright red. For the second time that morning, I wanted to run away and hide.

But before I could make my escape, Mr. Ship stood up from the piano and said, "It seems we have a new student. One with an outstanding voice. What's your name?" he asked.

"Amy Hodges," I said in almost a whisper.

"Well done, Amy Hodges," he said.

"Thank you," I whispered, looking at the floor.

I could still feel everyone's eyes on me.

Mr. Ship sat back down at the piano and started playing the song again. I looked up real fast to see if anyone was still looking at me. Most of them weren't, but Jennifer and Liza were. They were standing with a girl from the other class. They had their arms folded in front of them and they were looking at me like I had done something wrong.

I looked away, quickly. It didn't matter how much Mr. Ship liked my singing. All I could think about were those three girls and how they didn't like me. I just didn't know why.

Chapter 5

When music class was over, everybody hurried off to lunch. But I walked slowly down the hall instead. I had no reason to rush. It's not like I had anyone to sit with.

When I walked through the cafeteria doors, my eyes opened wide. It looked as if the entire school was already there. And I couldn't believe how loud it was. Some of the kids were lined up to get their lunch and some were already sitting down eating. Everyone was talking and laughing and having fun. Everyone except me.

Since Mom had packed a lunch for me, I didn't need to stand in line. So I slowly walked around looking for a place to sit. But there were kids at every single table. And it felt like every one of them was staring at me.

I started to panic. Where was I going to sit? Maybe I could just go back to my classroom and eat. At least it was quiet in there.

"Hey, you're a really good singer," someone called out.

I looked up and saw the girl wearing the roller-coaster T-shirt that had been at the bus stop. She was holding a lunch tray in her hands.

"Thanks," I said.

She laughed. "But that dress has got to go!" It wasn't a mean kind of laugh, though. Not like Jennifer and her friends.

I looked down at my dress. It was true. Compared to what everyone else was wearing at school, my dress *was* way too fancy.

I smiled. Finally, someone was being nice to me.

"Why are you just standing there?" the girl asked. "Come sit with us."

When we got to her table, she handed me a white sweater.

"Here, wear this," she said. "It'll cover that hole."

"Thanks," I said, pulling on her sweater. "I'm Amy."

"I'm Lola," she said. "And you're welcome."

I looked at her roller-coaster T-shirt again. "Did you really ride the Monster Loop?" I asked.

"Four times," she said proudly.

"Wow! I'd never be brave enough to do that," I said.

"Never say never," Lola said with a smile as she sat down.

There were two boys sitting at the other end of the table. "That's my twin brother Cole," Lola said, pointing. "And that's Rusty."

Rusty turned around. He was wearing a pair of joke glasses—the kind that have eyeballs that pop out on springs.

"Hey, Lola," he said as the eyes bobbed up and down. "I've been keeping an eye out for you!" Then he and Cole burst out laughing.

"He thinks he's such a comedian," said Lola.

"Hi," I said.

Cole waved, and Rusty smiled with a big goofy grin.

"Hey," Cole said. I recognized him from the bus stop, too.

Rusty, who was in Mrs. Clark's class, too, said, "What's up?" But before I could answer, the boys went back to their conversation.

"Well, don't just stand there," Lola said, sitting down. "Sit."

I was feeling a little better now that I was wearing Lola's sweater. And that I had a place to sit with people who were being nice to me.

I sat down in the empty seat next to Lola and searched inside my backpack for my lunch. Yum. Mom had packed sushi!

I pulled the chopsticks out of my lunch bag and was just about to dig in when another girl from Mrs. Clark's class sat down at the table. She was wearing a lacy wrap shirt and beautiful sparkly hoop earrings. "What's up, Lola?" she asked.

"Amy, this is Pia," said Lola. "If you ever need any advice about what to wear, Pia's your girl!"

"Hi," I said to Pia. "Anyone want some of my sushi?"

"No way," said Lola. "I'm sticking to my turkey sandwich."

"Ohhh, I love sushi," said Pia. "I'll try a

teeny tiny piece, if that's okay."

"Here," I said, handing her some.

"Thanks," she said. Then she put the whole piece in her mouth and closed her eyes as she swallowed. "That's so good!"

"Yuck!" cried Lola.

Just then, two other girls sat down at the table. They were in the middle of a conversation.

One girl said, "Maya, how many times do I have to tell you, it's not fair for you to do all the work all the time." The girl talking sounded pretty bossy.

"I know, Jesse," the other girl said in a sweet voice. "But it's just one little book report. And I don't want to start any trouble."

"You're *too* nice," Jesse said.

Lola leaned forward, closer to Jesse. "What did Maya do now?"

Jesse sighed. "We're doing book reports in Mrs. Musgrove's class and we're supposed to work with a partner. Maya got stuck working with Gracie. And guess who isn't doing her share of the work?"

Lola nodded her head. "Gracie." Then she turned to me and said, "Oh! Maya, Jesse, this is Amy."

"Hey," said Jesse.

"You were great in music class. I wish I knew how to sing like that," Maya said.

"Oh, I'm not *that* good," I said, shaking my head.

Pretty soon everyone at the table was eating

and talking and laughing. Well, Jesse did most of the talking, really. This was just the way I had wished school would be.

Just then, I noticed that Liza, Jennifer, and the girl from the other class were all sitting at the table next to us. All three girls were looking right at me. Then Jennifer leaned over to Liza and said loudly, "The new girl looks kind of *weird*, right? What *is* she, anyway?"

Liza and the other girl shrugged their shoulders and started laughing.

Before I could control it, tears filled my eyes. First they had made fun of my dress, then they made fun of my singing, but this was different. Now they were making fun of who I was. My family. It wasn't right.

Jesse leaned over to me. "Don't pay any attention to Jennifer," she said. "She and her friends Liza and Gracie are jerks, if you ask me."

But I was too upset to speak.

"Jesse is right," Lola said. "When Cole and I moved here, Jennifer said some mean things about us, too. Remember, Cole?"

Cole looked up. "Yeah. She called us the mixed-up twins."

I tried to blink my tears away. "Mixed up?" I asked.

"Yeah," he said. "Because we're mixed. Biracial. Our mom is black and our dad is white."

Pia nodded. "Jennifer said something mean about me, too. My mom is white and my dad is Chinese. My parents said I should just ignore people like Jennifer."

"Our mom and dad tell us that, too," Lola said. "Anyway, a lot of kids are mixed. Jesse is black and Puerto Rican. And Rusty is Latino, Native American, and white."

I had never been around kids who had lots of different cultures in their family like I had. Finally! I wasn't the only one. "I'm black, white, Japanese, and Korean," I told everybody.

Lola giggled. "Wow! Your name shouldn't be Amy Hodges. It should be Amy Hodgepodge!"

Everyone laughed and so did I. Laughing and

being around people like me made me feel a lot better. It was enough to make me forget about Jennifer. Well, almost.

The rest of the day went by so fast. Before I knew it, I was back on the school bus going home. When the bus reached my stop, I looked out the window and saw Mom standing there with Giggles. I jumped up and almost ran off the bus. I gave Mom a big hug. Then I knelt down to hug and pet Giggles. I had missed him so much.

When everyone got off the bus, I introduced Mom to Lola, Cole, Pia, Maya, and Jesse. Rusty didn't take our bus because he didn't live in Maple Heights. He lived all the way on the other side of town.

"Hi, kids," Mom said, cheerfully.

"I'll see you tomorrow," I said as I waved good-bye to everyone.

"See you later, Amy Hodgepodge," Lola said as she turned to walk down the block.

Mom handed me Giggles's leash. Then she

asked, "Why did your new friend Lola call you Amy Hodgepodge?" Mom asked.

I laughed. "It's just a joke."

"And where did you get this sweater?" she asked.

"Oh, that." I didn't want to tell her about Liza and Jennifer and how they had made fun of my dress, so I just said, "I accidentally ripped my dress, so I borrowed it from Lola." It wasn't a complete lie.

"I'm so glad you made friends so easily," Mom said.

I didn't say anything. I just let Giggles pull me along a little faster. Lola and all of her friends were probably just being nice to me because I was the new kid. I didn't know if they were really my friends yet.

That night at dinner, everyone asked me a million questions about my first day of school.

"My teacher, Mrs. Clark, is really nice," I told them. "And we have a hamster and goldfish in our classroom."

My family listened as I spoke, but I got the feeling that they still weren't one hundred percent happy that I had decided to go to school. They didn't seem to understand how important this was to me.

My grandfather poured more tea for my grandmother and said, "It sounds like you had a wonderful day, Amy."

"I did, Harabujy," I said, swallowing hard. It felt terrible not telling my family about the bad things that had happened. But if I told them about what Rory did or what Liza, Jennifer, and Gracie said about me, my parents might not let me go back to school.

Yes, my first day of school had been really hard, but I still wanted to go back. I didn't want to give up so easily.

So I had no choice. I just wouldn't tell them everything.

Chapter 6

The next morning I dressed in jeans and a pretty red T-shirt with little hearts on it. I didn't want to give Jennifer and her friends any reason to tease me.

Right before lunch, Mrs. Clark told everybody to quiet down because she had a big announcement.

"Class," Mrs. Clark said. "Emerson will be holding a talent show in two weeks, and all of you are welcome to take part in it."

Everyone cheered. Everyone except me. A talent show? I had never done anything like that before. The thought of getting on a stage in front of an audience seemed way too scary. I had freaked out when everyone heard me sing in music class, and that was *nothing* compared to an entire auditorium full of people!

"You can perform alone or in groups, but you need to let me know if you plan to participate as soon as possible."

Right away, everybody started moving around the room. Two boys high-fived each other. "We're going to rock!" one boy said.

"No," the other said. "We're going to *rock and roll!*"

Lola and Pia were also talking. I couldn't hear what they were saying, but I could tell they were talking about the talent show. And they both looked thrilled about it.

In front of me, Liza leaned over to Jennifer and said, "Isn't this great? We can work together again."

Jennifer nodded. "I don't know why everybody else is getting excited when we're *definitely* going to win again."

"*Definitely*," Liza agreed.

When we left class to go to lunch, everyone was still talking about the talent show. Everyone seemed to know who they were going to work with. Everybody except me. I was all alone. Again.

In the cafeteria, I watched as Lola and Pia headed straight for their table in the middle of the room where all of their friends were waiting. There were empty seats, but I didn't know if I should sit with them. They were all really nice to me yesterday, and we talked a little bit at the bus stop that morning, but they all seemed to be very close friends. Maybe they didn't want anybody else to join their group.

So I found a seat in the back of the cafeteria and pulled out my tuna sandwich. Sitting alone wasn't so bad, I told myself. Anyway, if I was sitting with them, all they would probably talk about was the stupid talent show.

I was halfway through my sandwich when Lola walked over to my table. "Hey, Amy, we've been looking for you. Why are you eating over here?"

I shrugged. "I dunno. I thought you guys
wanted to eat by yourselves."

"You're crazy," Lola said, picking up my
backpack for me. "Come on."

I couldn't help smiling really big. "Okay." I
grabbed my lunch and walked with her back
to her table. And just as I expected, they were
talking about the talent show and nothing else.

"Let's form our own group," Jesse said. "We'll
sing *and* dance." She sounded like she was in
charge.

"I know how to break-dance," Rusty said from the other end of the table.

Cole folded his arms in front of him. "Since when?" he asked.

"Since my cousin Luis taught me some moves," Rusty answered.

"Okay," Jesse said. "We'll all sing and dance. And Rusty will break-dance. The crowd will flip out when they see Rusty break-dance. No one's ever done anything like that in the talent show before. And I'm going to be the lead singer."

"That would be great, except for one thing," said Lola with a giggle. "You can't sing!"

"Yes, I can!" Jesse shot back. "I'll prove it. I'll sing and then you all can vote on if I'm good enough."

Jesse only managed to sing a few words before Cole and Rusty covered their ears.

"I vote we lock Jesse's mouth shut," said Cole with a smile.

"And launch the key into outer space," added Rusty.

"Then bury it on planet Mars," said Lola.

"Then blow up Mars with a giant missile," added Pia.

We were all laughing now, even Jesse.

"Okay, okay. I get it," said Jesse.

Just then, Lola turned to me. "Oh, Amy. You *have* to sing lead. You have one of the best voices in our class."

They wanted me? How cool was that? Now I didn't just have to watch!

"Yeah," Jesse reluctantly agreed with Lola. "You'll sing lead and we'll be your backup singers." But the way she said it made me feel

like I didn't even have a choice.

"With your voice, Amy," Pia said, "we'll definitely get that trophy!" Her eyes lit up brightly.

Everyone nodded excitedly, but my stomach was flipping around like a circus acrobat. At first all this seemed like a good idea, but now I had to find a way to get out of this. There was no way I could sing lead in front of an audience.

"Hey, are you okay?" Lola asked me.

"I don't know," I said, feeling all shaky inside. "I've never sung in front of an audience before. I—I'm not sure I can do it."

"Sure you can," Lola said. "We'll rehearse over and over until you're not nervous anymore."

"And we'll all be on the stage together," Maya said. "You're not going to be alone."

"You're going to do it, right, Amy?" Lola asked.

Everyone was staring at me. They wanted me to say yes, and I didn't want to let them all down. I really didn't. But I had to. "I can't," I whispered. "I'll be in the talent show with you, but I can't sing lead."

Everyone sighed loudly.

"That's okay, Amy," Lola said. "I'm sure your voice will help us, anyway, even if you just sing backup."

"Sorry, guys," I said. "I hope you understand."

"We understand," Maya said. And she looked like she did, too.

But she was probably the only one. Everyone else looked disappointed. All of their excitement was gone now. And it was all because of me.

Chapter 7

The next day, Lola and I headed to the cafeteria for lunch. Lola put her arm around my shoulders and said, "In case you didn't know, we want you to eat with us again. And the same goes for tomorrow and the next day and the next day."

"That's Saturday," I said, giggling.

"You know what I mean," she said, laughing.

As we walked together to "our" table, it felt so good to be part of the group. I wasn't sure this made me an official friend, but at least I was in the talent show with them. And that was a start.

After everyone was done eating, Jesse started making plans for the talent show.

"Okay, everyone," she said. "We need to start thinking about our routine."

Lola looked around the cafeteria. "Let's not talk about it here. We don't want anyone to copy our ideas, right?"

"You're right," Pia agreed. Then she turned to the rest of us. "Don't forget, guys. We want to win the trophy!"

Just then I heard someone say, "Trophy?"

I didn't need to see who had spoken. I knew it was Jennifer. She was sitting at the next table with Liza and Gracie. "Who are they kidding?" she asked, laughing a little bit.

"Hey, Jennifer, what's your problem?" Lola asked, folding her arms in front of her.

Jennifer stood up and came over to our table. Liza and Gracie followed her like they were her bodyguards. "*I* don't have a problem," Jennifer said. "*You* do. We won the trophy last year and we plan on winning it this year." She looked at each of us, one at a time. "If I were you, I wouldn't even bother competing in the talent show. You're just wasting your time."

She flipped her hair and walked back to her table.

"I can't believe that girl," Jesse said as Jennifer sat back down at her table. "She thinks she's so talented—"

"She *is* talented," Maya interrupted. "She does everything well. She can sing, act, and dance."

"Well, we have Amy Hodgepodge now," Lola said, "and her voice is going to make us sound a whole lot better."

"I wish Amy were singing lead," Pia said under her breath. "Then we'd win for sure."

There was a long silence. I moved around in my seat. I knew they wanted me to change my mind, but I couldn't. Just the thought of singing backup was scary enough.

"Sorry," I told them.

There were a few moments of silence. Then Lola said, "We can't let Jennifer get us down. We're going to do a great routine!"

"You're right," Maya agreed.

"Of course I'm right," Lola said. "Let's all meet at my house on Saturday. We can plan everything while we hang out in our tree house. It can be our official meeting place."

"Okay!" I said, having a hard time controlling my excitement.

This was going to be great. I was going to Lola and Cole's house on Saturday. This

was the kind of thing I had hoped for when I
convinced Mom and Dad to let me go to school.

Now I just had to figure out a way to survive
the talent show!

My Friends ♡

Jesse

School Spirit!!

She talks a
mile a minute!

Rusty

He's so funny!

Pia

She loves fashion!

Cole

Lola's twin brother!

Maya

Maya's sweet!

Lola

She was my first friend at school!

Chapter 8

On Saturday morning, Mom walked me and Giggles over to Lola and Cole's house. While Mom talked to Lola and Cole's parents, I took Giggles around to the back of the house.

I didn't know what to expect when Lola told me she and Cole had a tree house, but I wasn't expecting what I saw. The tree house was huge! It even had a slanted roof and windows and doors. The coolest part was the wooden ladder that was painted rainbow colors. All I could think was: *Wow!*

Everybody was already up in the tree house when I got there. They were making a lot of noise laughing. "Hey, Amy," Lola called down, leaning out of one of the windows.

I bent down to pet Giggles one last time before I went up to the tree house.

"What kind of dog is that?" Lola asked.

"Everyone calls Giggles a mutt because he's not just one kind of dog," I said.

"Cool," said Lola. "Well, come on up . . . and bring Giggles with you."

Once Giggles and I had climbed the ladder, I saw that everyone was sitting in a circle on the floor with their legs crossed.

"What a cute dog," said Lola. Giggles had headed straight for her and was now licking her hand.

"Your tree house is awesome," I told Lola and Cole.

"Thanks," Lola said. "Our dad built it when we first moved here."

"I helped," Cole said, proudly.

"Well, so did I," said Lola.

Jesse cleared her throat. "It's time to get started," she said. She had a yellow pad and pen in front of her. She was ready to get down to business!

I joined the circle and we all got right to work. Everybody had ideas. We knew we wanted to sing and dance. And Rusty knew he wanted to break-dance. But we had to figure out a way to make it all work together in the same song.

"Rusty could start the routine with his break-dance," Lola suggested.

Jesse shook her head. "No, we should sing first."

"Should we sing and dance at the same time?" I asked.

"No, that's going to be too hard," Cole said.

It wasn't easy getting all seven of us to agree, but after a while we came up with a plan. Maya

agreed to sing the lead even though she didn't think her voice was good enough. The routine would begin with Maya singing alone while everyone else sang backup and danced. Then, near the end of the song, Rusty would do his solo break-dance. But there was a lot of work to do!

"What are we going to sing about?" Lola asked.

"How about school?" Maya asked. "We could sing about the teachers and the cafeteria food and the homework and tests."

Everybody groaned.

"What about sports?" Rusty asked.

"Or movie stars!" Pia said, her face lighting up for the first time.

"Or dogs!" I said.

But everyone just stared at me. "Or . . . not," I said quietly.

"We're not getting anywhere," Jesse said, sighing. "We're all too different."

"I know," Lola said. "Can you believe that we're all friends?"

Everybody laughed, and I felt good being called one of the friends.

"That's it," Cole said, standing up and banging his head on a low part of the slanted roof. "Ow!"

We all giggled as he rubbed his head.

"We can sing about how everybody is different," he said.

"Yeah," Lola said, smiling. Everybody seemed to think that this was a good idea.

We decided to call the song "Celebrate You and Me." Cole found some cool music for us to sing to. Next all we had to do was write some lyrics and make sure they fit the beat.

We worked hard all morning and managed to come up with half of the song. We still had a lot of work to do, but it was time to take a break and eat some lunch.

While we were eating inside the house, Mrs. McCarthy said, "Kids, I need to pick up some groceries and your father isn't back from the gym. I don't want to leave you here all alone."

"We'll go with you, Mom," Cole said.

"Yeah," Lola added. "Maybe a long walk will help us think. And when we come back we can finish writing our song."

"And we can look in some of the stores for costumes," Pia said.

Lola shook her head. "Are clothes all you ever think about?"

"Kind of," Pia said, laughing.

I could tell it was true. Every day Pia showed up at school wearing all the coolest clothes. And she always looked perfect, like a movie star or model.

"Come on, kids," Mrs. McCarthy said, throwing her pocketbook over her shoulder.

I ran outside and got Giggles so he could come with us. Then we all walked over to Tisdale Street.

I had only been there twice with my parents, but Tisdale Street had all the best stores. My favorite store was called Lovem's Sweets-N-Treats because they sold candy and ice cream.

And there was an arcade right next door.

While Mrs. McCarthy went into the supermarket, she said it was okay if we stayed outside since they didn't let dogs into the store. So while we waited for her, we looked in a nearby store window trying to find something to wear in the talent show.

"Hey, what do you guys think of that?" Pia asked, pointing to a rack of overalls inside a store. "I think those could be our costumes."

"Great idea," I said.

"Yeah," Lola agreed. "And what about those T-shirts? The ones with the metallic design."

"That will look nice together," Pia said. "Our costumes are going to be the coolest."

Jesse stepped up to the glass door. "Come on, Pia. Let's go see how much everything costs."

While Jesse and Pia were inside the store, I pet Giggles for a little while. I didn't want him to think I had forgotten about him now that I had new friends. No matter what, he would always be my best friend.

When Jesse and Pia came back outside they told us that the costumes would cost $18.50 each.

"That's not too much," Lola said.

"Yeah," I agreed. "When I get home, I'll ask my parents if it's okay."

Everyone agreed to ask their parents, too.

The only person who didn't say anything right away was Rusty. He looked down at the ground.

"Rusty, do you like our costumes?" Lola asked him.

"Sure, pop star farmers are the coolest," said Rusty.

"What's with you, Rusty?" asked Lola. "Why are you being so mean? Those costumes are really nice."

"I don't know if I, um, really want to be in the show anymore," said Rusty.

Everyone looked shocked.

"What?!" Jesse asked. "If you really hate the costumes, we can change them."

Rusty shrugged his shoulders. "It's not that. Maybe all this is not a good idea," he said.

"Are you nuts? You have to do it!" said Jesse.

"Yeah," added Pia. "What about your solo?"

"I changed my mind," said Rusty. "Just leave me alone, okay?"

We all looked at one another as Rusty walked away. It would be terrible if Rusty wasn't in the show with us. Especially since his solo break-dance was going to be our big ending. It was the thing the crowd was going to love!

When Mrs. McCarthy came out of the supermarket, she asked where Rusty had gone. As we all walked back to Lola and Cole's house, we explained how Rusty had suddenly acted so strangely.

When we got back to Lola and Cole's house, we got right back down to work. There was still a lot to do. Not only did we have to finish writing the song, but we had to work on our dance steps.

But none of it seemed like fun anymore. Even though nobody said it, they were all probably thinking the same thing I was. Without Rusty's solo break-dance, our routine would never win the talent show. Never.

Chapter 9

After rehearsal was done, my grandparents came to pick me up from Lola and Cole's house.

"So, did you have a good time?" my grandfather asked me as we walked home.

"Yes, Harabujy," I said, thinking about all the fun we'd had. We had written the whole song. And it was really good. We also started to work on our dance steps. But we ended up doing more laughing than dancing. That was fun.

But I couldn't stop thinking about Rusty and how he didn't want to be in the show anymore. And I thought about how everyone still wanted me to sing lead and how I was letting them all down. It was all too much.

"You look sad, Little Mitsukai," my grandmother said, grabbing my hand.

I sighed. "I'm okay, Obaasan." Then I decided to change the subject. I pointed to some flowers in somebody's garden and said, "Those are beautiful."

Just as I thought, my grandparents started talking about flowers. They decided to take the

long way home, just so they could see all the
different kinds of flowers in the neighborhood.
When I was homeschooled we used to walk
around and look at flowers all the time. And
when the weather was nice, we would even go
to the park to read or study.

I really missed being homeschooled. Things
were so simple then. It was like my whole life
had changed in a week.

We walked for a while without talking.
Then my grandfather asked, "Are you unhappy,
Amy?"

Suddenly, I felt tears in my eyes. And
my throat felt tight. I couldn't talk, so I just
nodded.

My grandfather put his arm around my
shoulders as we walked. "I thought you were
happy," he said. "You have so many friends
now."

"My friends are nice," I said through my
tears. "But I don't want to go back to school."

I knew I wasn't making any sense,

but I couldn't really help it. Luckily, my grandparents didn't ask me a whole lot of questions. They let me finish crying and then we went home. And that's one of the things I love about them. They know exactly what I need.

For the rest of the evening, I moped around the house. When Mom asked me to set the table for dinner, I mumbled under my breath, "I can't do everything."

But Mom heard me. "Everything like what?" she asked.

I thought about the talent show and how my friends and I probably wouldn't win the trophy, not unless I sang lead. "Nothing," I said. "I was just thinking about something else."

"The talent show?"

I looked up at her. "How did you know?"

"I'm your mother. I can tell when something is bothering you." She handed me five plates and I started setting the table. "Are you having problems with the other kids?" she asked.

"No," I said. "I'm just nervous, that's all."

"Just do your best," Mom said. "You can't do any better than your best."

"I know." I put down the last plate and Mom handed me the silverware. As I finished setting the table I kept thinking about what she said. It did make me feel a little better. But was only singing backup really my *best*?

That night I stood in front of the mirror in my bedroom and sang along with the radio. Giggles was sitting on his doggie bed watching me. I was pretending to be a pop singer, and Giggles was my audience. And since I was a star, I was singing loudly, and with extra feeling and emotion.

"*I miss you, baby,*" I sang, swinging my head back and closing my eyes. "*Oh, I miss you.*"

There was a knock on my door, making me jump a little bit. "Come in," I yelled over the music.

Dad walked in.

"Oh, I'm sorry," I said before he could say anything. "Is my radio too loud?"

"Yes," he said, turning it down. "But that's not why I knocked."

"It's not?"

"I heard you singing," Dad said.

I immediately felt embarrassed. Dad had probably heard me sing a hundred thousand times before, but not like that. Not when I was pretending to be a superstar.

"You have a beautiful voice," Dad said, looking at me. "You should sing more often."

I shook my head. "I was just being silly for Giggles."

"You have a gift," he said. "Your voice reminds me of my mother's. Did you know she used to sing in the gospel choir at her church? She has a lovely voice."

"I didn't know Grandma Hodges sings."

He nodded. "Well, she doesn't sing too much anymore. But she did when I was growing up, and hearing you just now, it brought back a lot of memories. Is singing part of the reason you wanted to go to Emerson?"

I shrugged. "Maybe. I don't know. I think I just wanted to find out if I'm good at anything, like if there's something I should be trying."

He smiled. "I think I get it now."

Then he opened his arms and I gave him a hug.

"You can do anything you set your mind to," Dad said, kissing the top of my head. "You know that, don't you?"

"Yes," I said. "I know."

Later, I lay in bed, but I couldn't fall asleep. So I let Giggles sleep on my bed with me. As Giggles tried to snuggle with me I suddenly felt a pinch.

"Ouch!" I cried. "Giggles, you need a pedicure. Your paws feel like bear claws!"

Once Giggles was settled and his paws were tucked underneath him, I rubbed his soft fur. I thought about everything—school, my new friends, and especially the talent show. Dad was probably right. Maybe I did want to go to Emerson because I wanted to sing. But now that I had the chance to sing in front of a lot of people, I was too scared to do it.

It was weird. It seemed that everybody around me thought I could do anything I wanted to do. The only person who wasn't so sure was me.

Chapter 10

The next week raced by. Every day was filled with school and friends, and when I got home there was homework and long walks with my grandmother. After school on Friday, Mom and I went up to Tisdale Street to buy the costume for the talent show. Then on the way home she told me that she and my grandparents were going to come to the talent show.

"What about Dad?" I asked.

"He's going to try," she said. "But he may not be able to get off from work. The hospital has been very busy."

"Oh," I said, feeling kind of sad. I really wanted Dad to come to the show. I knew he'd be proud of me, even if I wasn't singing the lead. But Dad had an important job, and sometimes he couldn't do everything with the rest of us.

On Saturday, Mom walked me over to Lola and Cole's house. Most of the kids were already there, but they weren't in the tree house this time. Since we were going to work on our dance routine, we stayed on the ground.

I brought Giggles with me again, and as soon as we got there he started running around, trying to play with everybody.

"Why did you bring your dog again?" Jesse asked, frustrated. "We have work to do."

"He likes coming," I said, kneeling down to pet Giggles and calm him down.

"But he's just getting in the way," Cole said.

I fastened the leash to Giggles's collar. "C'mon, Giggles," I said and led him to the other side of the yard. I hooked the leash to the fence and whispered, "Pretty soon they'll all like you as much as I do. I promise."

"Okay, guys," Jesse said. "Let's stay on track. We have a lot of work to do before Friday—especially if Rusty's not going to be in the show anymore."

I wondered why Rusty suddenly didn't want to work with us. He had seemed so excited about doing his break-dance. What could have changed?

"Let's get started," Jesse said.

We all took our places on the grass and Cole pushed "play" on his mini boom box.

"Step, step, clap, turn," Jesse called out as we danced.

Cole was being so clumsy. He kept stepping on everyone's feet.

"Watch it, Cole!" shouted Jesse. "You're ruining the routine."

"I'm trying, I'm trying," said Cole.

It seemed like ever since Rusty quit the group, everyone had been really stressed out.

We danced for a little while, then we tried to sing and dance at the same time. Maya stood in the middle and started singing the beginning of the song alone. She did have a nice voice, but it wasn't very powerful. And she didn't really look like she was having any fun.

After about an hour and a half, Lola said, "Let's take a break. I'm thirsty."

"Okay," Jesse said. "But let's not take too long."

We all raced into the house. Singing and dancing really made you thirsty. We stood around drinking pink lemonade, but none of us looked all that happy. And I couldn't help feeling kind of guilty.

I knew Maya was trying her best to sing lead. And at least she wasn't scared to do it like I was. But without Rusty's break-dance, our routine was going to need something else to make it special. My voice was a lot stronger than Maya's and maybe if I sang lead, we would have a chance of winning. Maybe.

But I couldn't be sure. The show was in less than a week. It just seemed like everything was happening too fast. Way too fast!

❀ ❀ ❀

Later that day, my grandmother picked me up from Lola's house, and we took one of our nice, long walks around the neighborhood with Giggles.

As we were walking down Tisdale Street, we ran into Rusty. He was carrying a large garbage bag and I could tell from the rattling sounds that it was full of soda cans.

"Rusty!" I called out, excitedly.

"Hey, Amy," he said, looking a little embarrassed.

"Grandma," I said, "this is Rusty Vasquez. He's in my class."

"It's nice to meet you," Grandma said.

"Nice to meet you, too, ma'am," Rusty said politely.

"Rusty, where are you going?" I asked.

"To the recycling center."

"That's a big bag of cans," I said. "Where did you get all of them from?"

"Just from my house," he said, looking away.

"Really? You guys must drink tons of soda."

He didn't say anything for a few seconds. Then he said, "They're not really from my family. I've been collecting cans all week, from garbage cans all over Dyver City, and cashing them in for money."

"How come?" I asked.

"I'm trying to save up enough money to buy the costume for the show," he said. "I wasn't sure I'd be able to get enough, so I backed out of the show. I figured if I could somehow get the money, I could join back in."

For a while I didn't know what to say. Maybe we shouldn't have picked such an expensive costume. Maybe his family couldn't afford to buy it. At the same time, I thought it was really cool that Rusty was working hard to earn the money himself.

"Can I help?" I asked.

"Sure," he replied.

My grandmother took the leash from me and said, "I'll wait out here with Giggles."

Rusty and I walked inside the recycling center. As we cashed in the cans, he told me all about his family, how his father was a construction worker who was having a hard time finding a job. His mother was the only one who was working. Not only that, but Rusty had five brothers and sisters. It was too hard for his mother to give him money for a costume when there were more important things to buy— things the whole family needed.

"You could have told us about your family," I said. "We would have all understood."

Rusty nodded. "I know. I was just kind of embarrassed. You all live in Maple Heights and have big houses. But I don't. It's hard being different all the time."

"I know about being different!" I said, and laughed a little bit. "I'm the new kid, remember? The one who was homeschooled her whole life! How different is that?"

Rusty laughed with me. "Okay, I get it. We're all kind of different."

By the time we were done, Rusty had cashed in $4.35 worth of cans. "Great," he said. "That's $1.10 more than I need." He reached in his pocket and pulled out a lot of bills. "Finally! Now I have enough." He smiled, and I could tell that he was proud of himself.

"Let's go get your costume and then tell the

others that you're back in the show!" I said.

"Cool!"

When we came out of the recycling center I asked my grandmother if I could walk with Rusty down the block to the clothing store.

She agreed and waited with Giggles on a nearby bench.

"I'll be right back, Obaasan," I said.

As we walked to the store to get Rusty's costume, I said, "Rehearsal wasn't the same without you. We really need you in the group." Then I told him about Maya and how she was trying hard to sing the lead.

"It's not too late for you to sing lead, you know," he said. "A lot of people get stage fright, but they get over it. You might even have fun!"

"I know," I said, suddenly feeling kind of silly. Rusty had a lot more problems than I had, and he didn't give up. He found a way to solve them himself. "But what if I do it and my voice cracks or I faint or something? I would be *so* embarrassed," I said.

"Oh, you're not going to faint!" Rusty said, laughing. "And if you *do* faint, I'll catch you!" He stuck out his arm and flexed his muscle.

I laughed. "Thanks!"

"So, are you going to do it?"

I shook my head no. "Even with you there to back me up, I still don't think that I can."

"Come on, Amy Hodgepodge," Rusty pleaded. "If I can go all over town collecting dirty cans to pay for my costume, you can get up onstage and sing. There were times when I was embarrassed doing that, too."

I thought about what Rusty said. If he could stand to be embarrassed a bit, so could I. Besides, I didn't want to let my new friends down. And maybe he was right. I might even have fun once I was onstage.

"Okay. I'm in!" I told Rusty.

As I said the words, a little chill ran through my body. Could I really do this?

I guess I was going to find out.

Chapter 11

At school the next day, Rusty and I both shared the good news with the group—he was back in the show and I was going to sing lead! Everyone was so excited. And Maya seemed more than a little relieved that she didn't have to sing lead anymore. With me singing lead and Rusty back in the group, we were happy for the whole rest of the week. And the rest of the rehearsals went great!

Friday came so fast that I wasn't ready for it. I wasn't ready for the talent show, either. Part of me wanted time to freeze so I would never have to sing in front of the audience. The other part of me wanted to get the show over as quickly as possible.

The talent show was supposed to start at

four o'clock, so right after the dismissal bell, we all headed over to the auditorium, carrying our costumes in shopping bags. Backstage there was a whole lot of confusion. And most of the kids looked as nervous and shaky as I was. Actually, I looked the most nervous. My hands were all sweaty and my teeth were even chattering a little.

Angela, a girl in my class, was holding a piece of paper and mumbling something to herself. When she saw how freaked out I looked she came over and said, "Relax. I'm sure you're going to do fine. Don't worry."

"Good luck to you, too," I said, and we both smiled at each other.

We all wanted to win the trophy, but that didn't mean we couldn't be nice to one another.

Just at that moment I saw Jennifer, Liza, and Gracie. They were already dressed for the show, and their costumes looked like they cost a lot of money. *A lot!* Jennifer was wearing a beautiful white dress with a puffy bottom. Liza

and Gracie were wearing the exact same dress in pink. They looked like three princesses.

"Let's put on our costumes," Lola said, staring at Jennifer, too. "Remember, Amy, it's a *talent* contest, not a fancy-dress contest."

She was right. Costumes weren't everything. And our costumes were nice, too. I just hoped everyone would like overalls and T-shirts as much as the princess dresses.

After we were dressed, all seven of us stood together in one corner of the room. We waited around for about fifteen minutes until we heard Mr. Ship get on the microphone.

"I would like to welcome everyone to Emerson Charter School's talent show. We have some very talented kids waiting backstage. So, what I want to know is, are you ready?"

Everyone applauded. Their clapping was so loud, it sounded like everyone in the whole town was out there.

"Oh, my goodness," I said, suddenly feeling panicked inside. In just a few minutes, I would be out there singing in front of all those people. How did I get myself into this? What had I been thinking?

I couldn't see the audience from backstage, but I hoped my mother and my grandparents had made it on time. And I hoped Dad was able to get away from the hospital in time to see me.

The funny thing is, I never told my parents or grandparents that I had decided to sing the lead. I wanted to surprise them.

I took a deep breath and tried to blow out all

of my nerves. But as soon as I breathed back in, all the nerves came back in with the air. What was I doing? How could I do this?

"Amy, what's wrong?" Maya asked, putting her hand on my shoulder. "You look a little green."

I wanted to tell her I was fine, but I couldn't find the words. I wasn't fine. I was a mess.

Lola came over and gave me a big hug. "Remember, we're a team," she said. "We're all going to be up on that stage with you."

"And Amy," Rusty said, "don't forget, if you faint, I'm going to catch you!" He flexed his arm muscle again.

I started laughing, and across the room I heard Jennifer say loudly, "Oh, brother!"

I looked at her standing there with her hands on her hips. She was trying to look tough. We just had to be tougher, that was all!

"Okay, everyone," Mr. Ship said from the stage. "Our first student is Danny Kaja. He'll be singing a traditional song from India."

Everybody applauded as Danny made his way to the stage.

Although we couldn't see Danny from where we were backstage, we could hear him. Danny was from India and he spoke with a thick accent. But that didn't matter because, for the talent show, he sang a song in Hindi, his native language. Nobody knew what he was singing about, and I had never heard that kind of melody before. But I think everyone was surprised by how beautiful his song was.

When he was done and the applause ended, Mr. Ship got back on the microphone. "Thank you, Danny. That was wonderful. Next we have Angela Chapman. She will be reading a poem that she wrote."

Angela looked so confident as she went onto the stage and began reading a poem about a time that she and her parents volunteered to help families who had lost their homes in a terrible hurricane.

Angela ended her poem by saying:

"The work was really hard,
But I did whatever I could
And I learned that helping other people,
Can make you really feel good!"

When she was finished, the whole audience gave her a standing ovation.

"That was great, Angela," I told her when she returned backstage. "You didn't seem nervous at all when you were out there."

"Are you kidding?" she said, shaking her head. "I thought I was going to throw up!"

She and I both laughed together.

Next Mr. Ship called Jennifer, Liza, and Gracie to the stage. Even before they did anything, everybody clapped very loudly. It was probably just because of their dresses and how they looked like real pop stars.

"Let's watch them," Pia said, and we all ran over to the side of the curtain where we could peek out and see their routine.

As soon as the music started, we recognized it from the radio. It was called "Listen to Me" and it was a big hit song. Jennifer started singing and I realized that what everybody had said about her was true. She did sing well. *Really* well.

"*I have a story to tell you,*" she sang in a beautiful soprano voice. "*Listen to me. Listen to me.*"

But when they began dancing, all of us opened our mouths in surprise. "They're just copying," I whispered.

"I know," Jesse said. "They're doing the exact same dance steps from the music video."

"That's not fair," Cole said.

"Yeah," Maya added. "They should have come up with something original."

"There's nothing original about them," Pia said, shaking her head.

But there were no rules about not using your own original song and dance moves.

When Jennifer, Liza, and Gracie finished performing, everybody clapped. Very loudly. Nobody seemed to care that they hadn't come up with their own song and dance.

Mr. Ship came back on the microphone. "We have another group coming out next," he said. "Please welcome Lola, Cole, Pia, Maya, Rusty, Jesse, and Amy."

My heart stopped for a few seconds. But I didn't have time to think. Lola grabbed my hand and we all ran out onto the stage and took our places. Since I was now singing lead, I was standing in the middle. As I stood there, I looked out at the audience. Every single seat was taken. It made me feel a little dizzy. I looked in the crowd for my parents and grandparents and spotted them right before the music began. And my father was there, too. He had made it. Yes!

Then the music started and everybody began dancing. I was a little late, though. And it took me a few seconds to catch up with the rest of them.

Then I had to sing, *alone*, but when I opened my mouth, my words came out too softly. I was sure most people couldn't even hear me. *"We are all special,"* I sang. *"That's plain to see."*

I could tell by the audience's reaction that I was bombing—big-time! Just when I thought that I would pass out from embarrassment, the rest of the group started singing.

They were helping me sing the part I was supposed to do alone! Their voices calmed me down a little bit, and right then I really felt like I was part of a team. I wasn't alone. *"So let's take the time, to celebrate you and me!"* we all sang.

Slowly, my voice became loud and clearer and right on pitch. Once the rest of the group could tell that I was feeling more confident, they started singing just backup.

I managed to sing the rest of the solo by myself—and I actually think I did pretty good. Then when we got to the chorus, we all sang and danced together, just the way we had rehearsed:

"Celebrate me,
Celebrate you,
Celebrate your talents,
And everything you do.

Celebrate you,
Celebrate me,
Celebrate your life,
And your family.

We're all one of a kind,
And you must agree
To take a little time,
To celebrate you and me!"

By the time Rusty stepped up to the front of the stage to do his break-dance, all I felt was happiness. I was in front of a huge crowd, but I wasn't scared anymore. The words to the song and being up there with my new friends were making me feel better.

And Rusty was great! He did everything, even a spin on his back like an upside-down turtle and a backflip. When he was done, he got a huge applause!

Now it was hard to believe that I had let Jennifer make me feel bad about myself. Even for one second. She could tease me all she wanted, but that didn't matter. I had a great family *and* great new friends who really liked me. And now I had school, too.

When our song was finished, we all took a bow while the audience applauded. Mom, Dad, and my grandparents were all standing up and cheering. And that felt great!

We ran off the stage, jumping up and down with excitement. Then when we got backstage, we all hugged and laughed. "That rocked!" Lola said, throwing her hands in the air.

"Yeah," said Rusty. "For a minute there, Amy, I thought you swallowed a bug. But then you really came through."

I felt tingly all over. But I couldn't talk.

I just knew that singing with my new friends in front of my family and all those people was going to be something I'd remember my whole life.

Chapter 12

Later, after everyone had performed, it was time to announce the winner. We were still so happy, we had almost forgotten it was a contest. Jennifer and her friends were on the other side of the room, and even though they all kept glaring at us, we barely noticed.

Mr. Ship got on the microphone again and thanked all of us who had participated in the talent show. "We will start with the third-place winner," he said.

We all huddled together to hear the names.

Mr. Ship continued, "The third-place winners are Jennifer, Liza, and Gracie!"

We all turned to look at them just in time to see the shocked look on Jennifer's face. *"Third place!"* she shrieked. *"Third place?"*

"Come on, Jennifer," Liza said, pulling her onto the stage.

When they came back, they were holding ribbons. Liza and Gracie seemed happy, but Jennifer was mad.

"Okay," Mr. Ship said. "Our second place winners are Lola, Cole, Pia, Maya, Rusty, Jesse, and Amy. Come on out, kids."

Even though I heard our names, it took me a few seconds to understand what he was saying. Then I shouted, "That's us!"

I was so excited when we all ran onto the stage to get our ribbons. When we left the stage, we hugged and laughed again. We hadn't won the trophy, but it was almost as good.

Angela won first place and the trophy. And she deserved it. When Mr. Ship called her name, everyone in the audience gave her another standing ovation. And we all cheered, too.

When the judging was over and we were back in our regular clothes, we all ran out to the lobby, where our parents were waiting for us. We all got tons of hugs and kisses. Mom was the first person to hug me. "I can't believe that was you up on that stage singing so beautifully," she said.

"Neither can I," I told her, laughing.

Then my grandparents handed me a bouquet of beautiful flowers. I was so happy. It was the first time I'd ever received flowers before.

"You were wonderful," my grandfather said, hugging me.

My grandmother nodded her head. "You sang like an angel."

I giggled, "Well, I am your Little Mitsukai, aren't I?"

"Yes," she said. "You certainly are."

Dad came over and gave me a big hug. "I am so proud of you, Amy," he said. "Now, wasn't that a lot better than singing in front of your mirror at home?"

"Like a million times better!" I said, feeling proud of myself, too.

Just then Rusty came over. "Hey, let's all go celebrate with ice cream!" he said.

That just got the rest of us singing again. *"Celebrate you, celebrate me,"* we sang, laughing the whole time.

Rusty chanted, "Ice cream! Ice cream!" as we all asked our parents if we could go.

Once everyone agreed, we all headed for the exit. On the way out, we couldn't stop talking about how much fun we had performing and how great it was to win ribbons. I also couldn't stop thinking about what a great scrapbook page I'd be able to make about the talent show. There'd be some great photos for me to put in of us performing—and of course, the ribbon that each of us had won. I just knew that once I made the page, I would be able to look back and remember how hard we had all worked. And how great I felt being part of the group and facing my fears of singing in front of a big audience.

"We make a great team," Lola said.

I looked around at all of us, all different colors, all one of a kind. "We're not just a team," I said, giggling. "Look at us. We're a family."

Everybody cheered.

And we cheered and laughed and celebrated for the rest of the afternoon.

The Talent Show

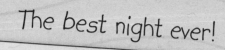

The best night ever!

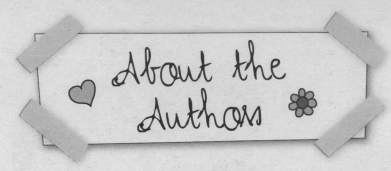

Kim Wayans and Kevin Knotts are actors and writers (and wife and husband) who live in Los Angeles, California. Kevin was raised on a ranch in Oklahoma, and Kim grew up in the heart of New York City. They were inspired to write the Amy Hodgepodge series by their beautiful nieces and nephews—many of whom are mixed-race children—and by the fact that when you look around the world today, it's more of a hodgepodge than ever.